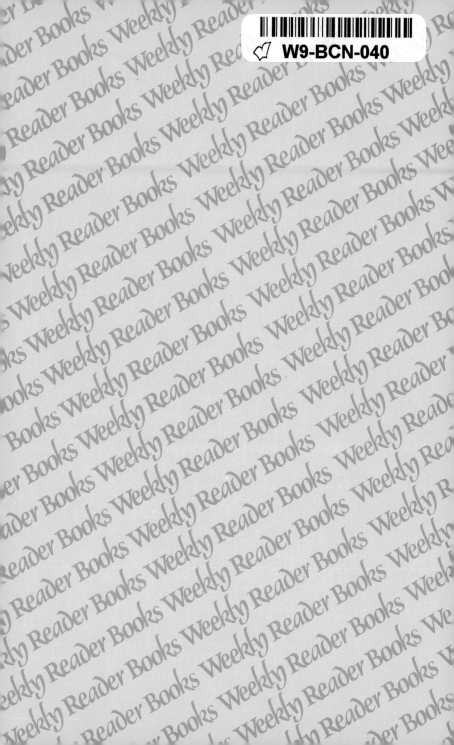

The Gismo

Also by Keo Felker Lazarus
The Gismonauts
A Message from Monaal

Weekly Reader Books presents

The Gismo

by Keo Felker Lazarus

Illustrated by Leonard Shortall

Follett Publishing Company

Editorial Offices: Chicago, Illinois

Regional Offices: Chicago, Illinois
Atlanta, Georgia • Dallas, Texas
Sacramento, California • Warrensburg, Missouri

The Library of Congress cataloged the first printing of
this title as follows:

Lazarus, Keo Felker.
    The gismo. Illustrated by Leonard Shortall. Chicago,
Follett Pub. Co. [1970]
    126 p. illus. 23 cm.
    Two boys discover that the unusual device they have found
is a communications system for a space ship enabling them to
contact men from another planet.

    [1. Science fiction]   I. Shortall, Leonard W., illus.
II. Title.
PZ7.L448Gi   [Fic]   75–118924
ISBN 0–695–80145–7   MARC

                     71 [4]   A C

Contents

1

What is it?

When Jerry Cole rode his bike home from Bridgeville Junior High, he pedaled furiously down School Street. At the first corner he thumbed the handlebar shift lever to high, back pedaled a second, and leaned right into Elm Street.

The wind combed his red hair straight back and roared in his ears. He liked to imagine he was the pilot of a jet plane or flying saucer zooming through space at a zillion miles an hour. For one block he pumped rapidly, then leaned into Park Lane, swung out of the bike seat, and rode the pedal up the driveway of the third house on the right.

Jerry arrived home from school every afternoon in exactly seven minutes ... every afternoon that is, except Thursdays.

On that day he took his time and rode home slowly by way of the alley that ran for three blocks behind all the important stores in Bridgeville. Thursday afternoons the shopkeepers put the trash out for the early Friday morning collection. Hal's Hobby Shop threw lots of good boxes away, and sometimes broken models from do-it-yourself kits. Gormley's Radio and TV Clinic dumped old radio tubes and capacitors into the foam packing of big television cartons. Jerry always checked through these cartons of trash. You never knew when Mr. Gormley might discard a broken transformer, a few usable lengths of solder, or those tiny plastic boxes certain radio parts came in. Now that Jerry was interested in building radios himself, he could use such items.

This Thursday afternoon Ron Baily, his best friend, rode beside him. Ron, who was in the seventh grade with Jerry, lived next door. They guided their bikes slowly down the alley, eyeing each trash bin they passed. At Gormley's they squeezed the hand brakes on their bikes, knocked the kickstands down, and began to rummage in the foam packing of a large discarded television carton.

"Wow! Look at this!" Ron exclaimed. "A whole spool of wire! Why would he throw *that* away?"

"Here, let me see." Jerry took the spool. He half closed his blue eyes, and squinted at the spool, turning it over in his hands. He wrinkled his freckled nose. "It's corroded on one side, that's why." He tossed the spool back to Ron.

"So what?" Ron caught the spool and flipped his shaggy black hair from his round face. "I can still use it." He stuffed the spool into his jeans.

Jerry tugged at a length of spaghetti tubing. It popped out of the carton, and he inspected it closely. It was split down one side. He threw it back. "I guess Mr. Gormley hasn't had much business this week . . . no decent junk," Jerry said and scuffed along the alley in the shadow of the power-line pole that stood behind Hal's Hobby Shop. Next to the pole there was a rusty oil drum stuffed with papers and boxes. In the first box he opened, he found half a plastic gemini space capsule model. But although he rummaged deep among the papers and boxes, he couldn't find the other half. He threw the plastic back into the trash. "Nothing here, either," he said. "Come on, let's go home."

Jerry flipped the kickstand up on his bike and was about to swing his leg over the seat when out of the corner of his eye he caught a metallic gleam. It came from the weeds along the alley—a spot halfway between the television carton and the metal trash barrel. Jerry leaned his bicycle against the power-line pole, walked over and lifted the tiny metal object from the ground. It was rectangular, the size and shape of a domino. Tiny knobs extended from either end and a third knob from one side. It felt slippery, like a quarter covered with quicksilver, yet it was light as balsa wood. The upper surface was covered with short, silver-colored brushlike wires. Jerry touched them. The wires felt soft and silky as fur.

"Ron! Come here!" Jerry cradled the tiny object in his hand.

Ron dropped a broken television knob back into the trash and loped to Jerry's side. He put his plump hands on his knees and peered closely. "What is it?"

"Search me!" Jerry said. "Maybe it's a

modular circuit from a transistor radio." He had heard the older boys in electric shop talking about modular circuits, but he hadn't seen one yet.

Ron shook his head. "Nope, it's not that. Remember when I dropped my transistor radio through the bleachers at the football game last week and it smashed all to pieces?"

"Yeah?"

"Well, it had a modular circuit and nothing like this gismo fell out of it. Say, aren't those wires moving?"

Jerry drew the object away from Ron's face. "You're breathing on them, that's why. Man! I'd sure like to know what this gismo is!"

Ron put his hands in his hip pockets. "Hey! I'll bet it came off one of those remote control planes . . . like the one in Hal's window."

"Yeah!" Jerry opened his hand and looked at the gismo more closely. He could see no visible seams or screws holding it together.

Ron reached into his pocket. "I'll trade you this spool of wire for it."

Jerry grinned and shook his head. "Nothing doing! I'm keeping it!"

"Why?"

"It's something I can use, that's why!"

Ron mounted his bike. "How can you use it if you don't know what it is?"

Jerry slipped the gismo into his right-hand pocket and climbed on his bike. "Don't worry, I'll find out what it is!"

When he coasted his bike up the driveway, his eight-year-old sister, Dodie, was slamming a rubber kickball against the garage door. The ball bounced back and hit his bike. Jerry reached down and grabbed the ball. He leaned his bike against the maple tree by the front porch, tucked the ball under his arm, and loped around the corner of the house toward the back door.

Dodie flipped her red braids over her shoulders and started after Jerry. "You give that back, Jerry Cole!"

Jerry ran ahead of her keeping just out of reach until he came to the back steps, then he looped the ball over her head. It hit the garage wall with a bang and bounced away onto the front lawn.

Dodie stamped her foot. "Brothers!" she exclaimed, and ran after the ball. Jerry slammed through the back door into the kitchen, fragrant with baking.

"Hi, Mom," he greeted his mother who was taking a pan of cookies from the oven. He closed his eyes and sniffed loudly. "Don't tell me—*peanut butter*! Right?" He opened his eyes.

His mother smiled. "Right!" She handed him a hot cookie on the end of the spatula.

"Thanks." Jerry tossed the cookie back and forth in his hands to cool it, then popped it into his mouth and munched loudly. He wiped his greasy hands on his jeans and felt the gismo in his pocket. He pulled it out. "Ever see a gismo like this, Mom?"

His mother slipped a second pan of cookies in the oven. "What's a gismo?" she asked.

Jerry reached for more cookies. "Oh *you* know! It's a—a gadget, a—a thing!" He stuffed a cookie into his mouth. "Have any idea what this is used for?"

His mother took the gismo and turned it over. "Is it a brush of some kind?"

"Don't think so—not with those knobs on the ends."

Mrs. Cole handed it back. "I'm not a very good guesser, Jerry. Ask Dad when he comes home tonight. He'll probably know."

Jerry stuffed a few more cookies into his pockets, and tossing the gismo into the air, started through the hall. His older sister, Lou, just turned fourteen, lay on her back across the hall runner. She was talking on the telephone. Jerry pretended not to see her and raised his foot as though to step on her stomach.

Lou let out a little screech and grabbed his foot. "Jerry Cole! You stop that!" She gave his leg a twist and threw him off balance. Jerry fell, knocking the telephone out of Lou's hand. The gismo slithered across the floor.

"Hey, Mom!" Jerry yelled, "Who left a rolled-up rug in the hall for people to fall over?"

"You little monster!" Lou exclaimed. She pushed him away and reached for the telephone. "Not you, Linda," she said into the phone, "this stupid brother of mine!"

Jerry got to his knees. "I've lost my gismo."

"Your *what*?" Lou asked.

"Ah, here it is!" Jerry reached behind the leg of the telephone stand. He sat back on his heels and stroked the gismo's silky wires.

Lou sat up. "Is that thing alive?"

"Yeah!" Jerry snaked the gismo along the floor toward Lou.

Lou jumped to her feet. "Mother—r—r, Jerry's got a mouse or something in here!"

Mrs. Cole came into the hallway. "That's enough, Jerry," she said sternly. "And Lou, tell Linda good-bye. I want you to set the table for supper."

Jerry stood up and clumped toward the stairs. "Sisters!" he muttered to himself.

After dinner, Jerry brought the gismo into the living room. His father was watching a local newscast about a recent UFO sighting near Bridgeville.

Jerry sat down on the couch beside his father. "Man! I'd sure like to see one of those UFO's close up, wouldn't you, Dad?"

Mr. Cole smiled. "If there's anything to see . . . They could be optical illusions, ionized air plasmas, or . . ."

Jerry grinned and leaned back. ". . . or swamp gas. Yeah, I know." He stuck his hands into his pockets and felt the gismo. He drew it out. "Ever see anything like this before, Dad?"

His father reached over and took the gismo. He turned it over slowly. "No, I haven't, Jerry, what is it?"

"That's what I'd like to know!"

"Where did you get it?"

"I found it near the trash barrel behind Gormley's."

Mr. Cole handed the gismo back. "Why

don't you ask Mr. Gormley. If he threw it away, he'd know what it is."

Jerry rolled the gismo in his hand. "It might have come from Hal's Hobby Shop, too. He's right next door to Gormley's."

Mr. Cole rose and switched the television off. "Well, ask Hal, too." He smiled at Jerry. "There's always a logical explanation for things like that. They don't simply fall out of the sky."

"Off that UFO, maybe?" Jerry grinned.

Mr. Cole tousled Jerry's hair. "With an imagination like yours, Son, you're bound to find out what it is!"

2

A strange voice

The next afternoon Jerry leaned his bike against the maple tree and ran for the back stairs. His trip to the TV Clinic and Hal's Hobby Shop had been fruitless. He scuffed into the kitchen and opened the refrigerator door. He stood looking in.

"Jerry," his mother called from the hall, "close the refrigerator door, please."

"I'm hungry," Jerry called back.

"Then help yourself to apples. And Jerry,

17

did you put your bike away in the garage?"

"I'll do it later, Mom." Jerry reached for two apples, slammed the refrigerator door, and ran upstairs to his room. He kicked the door shut with one foot and plopped down on his bed.

The crystal radio set he had made at school was on his nightstand. His pocket transistor was there too, but it was more fun to fool with the crystal set. Now for some quiet relaxing music, Jerry thought. He placed one apple on the stand, and with the other apple between his teeth, he picked the headphones up and adjusted them over his ears. He checked the aerial that ran behind his bed through the window screen to the top of the maple tree. Yes, it was attached securely. He glanced at the ground wired to the heating duct close by. It was in place, too. Then he reached for the crystal radio and moved the tuner bar across the coil until he heard the voice of a disk jockey on the local radio station.

He leaned his head back on his pillow and crunched into the apple while he listened to the beat of a new tune. He put his hand into his jeans pocket, pulled the gismo out, and rolled it between his fingers and palm. He liked the slippery feel of it. Placing the gismo on the pillow beside him, he turned his head and stared

18

at the tiny knobs on the ends and one side. What had it been attached to, he wondered . . . wires? . . . clips? Did it fit into a slot? Was it a cartridge of some kind? And those fine hair-like wires on top! Were they antennae? He blew on them and they parted like the fur on a cat. Hal had said it might have come from a telephone truck or a lineman's pocket. If so, it could have something to do with a telephone. Maybe it was a relay of some kind, or a new type of transformer.

Jerry took another bite of apple. Funny how grown-ups like Mr. Gormley, and even Hal, gave up so easily. He'd have to figure out the secret of the gismo himself.

Somebody was thumping on his door. "You there, Jerry?" It was Ron.

"Sure, come on in." Jerry took the ear-phones off.

Ron walked in. "Your mom said it was okay to come up."

Jerry reached for the apple on his night-stand. "Here, catch!" He lobbed the apple at Ron.

Ron caught it as it hit his stomach. "Thanks," he said and bit into the apple. He flopped down on the foot of the bed. "Whatcha doing?"

"Fooling around with the gismo."

"Got any ideas what it is yet?"

"Well, it isn't a TV part."

"How do you know?"

"Gormley said so. Picked up a couple of alligator clips at his store after school."

"Then I'll bet it's a model-airplane motor like I said."

Jerry shook his head. "Hal said it wasn't that, either. He looked it over real good." Jerry picked the gismo up and turned it over in his hand. It doesn't come apart . . . no screws . . . no seams . . . nothing. These knobs on the ends and sides . . . maybe something was attached to them."

"What, for instance?" Ron leaned back on the bed and munched loudly.

"Electric wires, maybe, like Hal said."

"For what?"

"Oh, anything. It might be a battery of some kind, you know."

"Yeah? How can you tell?"

Jerry sat up. "Remember in electric shop when we learned how batteries worked?"

"Sure, I remember."

"Well, if this gismo is a battery, I could attach wires to the little knobs on it, then touch the wires to a flashlight bulb, and the bulb would light up."

"Okay, let's try it." Ron sat up.

Jerry hurried to his desk, cluttered with bits of wire and parts of old radios. He rummaged about in one of the drawers and found his flashlight. Removing the glass from the front, he unscrewed the tiny bulb. He selected a short wire from his desk and wound one end of it carefully about an end knob on the gismo. The other end of the wire, he wound about the brass threads of the bulb. He found a second wire on his desk and fastened one end to the other end knob on the gismo.

He brought it over to the bed. Ron held the gismo while Jerry carefully touched the free end of the wire to the dot of solder on the flashlight bulb. They looked closely. There was no glimmer of light.

"Maybe if you attached a wire to the side knob it would work," Ron suggested.

Jerry tried this, but still the bulb would not light.

Ron leaned back on one elbow and tossed his apple core into the wastepaper basket across the room. It landed with a loud *thunk*. "Well, it isn't a battery," he said. "Got any other bright ideas?"

Jerry sat with his chin in his hands. "If it doesn't store electricity, maybe it conducts it. Remember when they showed us how a string of Christmas tree lights worked in a series?"

"Sure," Ron said. "If one bulb was loose or burned-out, the whole string wouldn't light."

"Yea, because a loose or burned-out bulb wouldn't conduct electricity." Jerry leaned forward. "Now if we connect this gismo in a series with something else, we can tell if it conducts." He went to his closet. "I've got my dry cell battery for starting model planes in here somewhere." He hunted among the boxes under his clothes and brought out a large, round battery. He carried it to his desk. Reaching into his jeans, he pulled the two alligator clips out.

Ron joined him at the desk with the gismo. Jerry removed the wires from the gismo and the light bulb and carefully attached a clip to each wire. He clamped the wires to the two terminals on top of the battery. The loose end of one wire he fastened to one end knob of the gismo. The loose end of the other wire he wound around the brass threads of the flashlight bulb.

He selected a third wire from his desk and attached one end of it to the other end knob of the gismo. "There!" Jerry put his hands on his hips. "The gismo's in a series." He leaned forward and touched the dot of solder on the light bulb with the free end of the third wire. The bulb didn't light. He tried again.

"Here," Ron said. "Let's try this." He removed the third wire from the end of the gismo and attached it to the side knob, then carefully touched the free end of the third wire to the dot of solder again. The bulb flickered a moment, then glowed softly. "Hey! It works!" Ron exclaimed. "It *does* conduct electricity!"

Jerry snapped his fingers. "Remember Hal said it might have fallen from a telephone truck?"

"Yeah?"

"Well, if it conducts electricity, maybe it conducts other things—like radio waves." He looked about his room. "If we could attach it to . . ." His eyes lit on the crystal radio set on his nightstand. "Hey! How about this?" Quickly he detached the gismo and hurried to the stand. He loosened the cat's whisker and crystal from the radio and fastened the gismo by its two end knobs in their place. He put the headphones over his ears and moved the tuner bar across the coil. There was a loud hum, but he couldn't tune in any radio stations.

Ron stood beside him. "What do you hear?"

"Nothing . . . just a hum."

Ron studied the set for a moment, then reached down and changed an end wire to the side knob of the gismo as he had done before.

Jerry jumped. "Wow!"

"What is it?" Ron asked eagerly. "Let me listen, too." He lifted the headphones from Jerry, turned one earphone so it faced outward, then put the set back on Jerry's head. Ron sat down next to Jerry and put his ear to the turned-out earphone. From the sputtering static a voice came in loud and clear. "XR . . . calling XR . . . come in, XR." The voice was high-pitched.

"You've got a ham radio band!" Ron exclaimed.

"On a crystal radio set?" Jerry glanced at the gismo, then caught Ron's arm. "Look at the gismo!" The tiny silver wires on top had become a faint pink color.

The voice came again. "XR . . . please report in." The wires on the gismo glowed cherry red as the voice spoke.

Jerry reached over and gingerly touched the glowing wires.

"Are they hot?" Ron asked.

"No, they feel cool." Jerry answered.

The voice began. "We have had no message from you since you entered the atmosphere of Planet Three, Sun G six zero eight, Syklo Galaxy."

Ron Chuckled. "Syklo Galaxy . . . that's

a good name for a science-fiction program. What station have you got?"

"I don't know." Jerry moved the tuner bar across the coil again, but only the humming came through.

The voice returned and the gismo glowed red. "Can you hear us, XR?" The voice sounded eager. "We're beginning to receive your transmitting signal now. Are you in trouble? We repeat: Are you in trouble?"

"Maybe we've hooked onto an airlines band." Ron said.

Jerry shook his head. "Airports and pilots don't talk about planets."

"This must be a gag of some ham operator," Ron said.

"XR . . . calling XR . . . your signal is clear now, but we're receiving no message. . . ." Repair craft are waiting for you at crater 7 del 5, natural satellite, Planet Three, Sun G six zero eight, Syklo Galaxy . . . over."

Jerry frowned. "That doesn't sound like a gag message to me. . . . That sounds like a real one from outer space."

Ron looked at Jerry in surprise. "It's got to be a gag! No one has cracked radio signals from outer space yet, let alone heard them in our own language!"

The gismo glowed as the high-pitched

voice broke in again. "XR . . . we repeat . . . repair craft are waiting for you at crater 7 del 5, natural satellite Planet Three, Sun G six zero eight, Syklo Galaxy . . . do you read us? . . . Over."

Jerry turned, and snapped his fingers. "I *know* this sounds crazy, but maybe it *isn't* a gag!"

"You've got to be kidding!"

"No, I'm not, Ron. Remember when we studied the solar system in Miss Mill's class?"

"Yeah?"

"She said billions of stars circle around in the galaxy we call the Milky Way. Remember the Greek name she used for it? Meant something like 'milky circle of stars,' I think."

Ron wrinkled his forehead. "Galax . . . *Galaxias Kyklos,* wasn't it?"

"Right! And doesn't that sound like 'Syklo?'"

"Yeah, but . . ."

"Miss Mills said our star, or sun, is out near the edge of the Galaxy and has nine planets circling around it." Jerry went on eagerly. "Earth is the *third planet from our sun.* Right?"

"Right."

Jerry leaned forward. "And what's the natural satellite of the earth?"

"The moon, of course," Ron said.

"And remember the report someone brought to school about astronomers seeing strange lights around one of the craters on the moon? And that UFO sighting near Bridgeville the other night?"

"What are you driving at, Jerry?"

"Oh, come on, Ron! Don't you get it? . . . UFO's . . . the moon. Earth's natural satellite with strange lights by a crater, maybe crater 7 del 5 . . . The earth . . . Planet Three . . . The sun . . . maybe number G six zero eight, to anyone that's counted all of them . . . and Syklo that sounds almost like Kyklos, the name for our own Galaxy. . . . Doesn't it add up?"

Ron looked at Jerry. "You mean this message could be for real? But from what?"

Jerry took the headphones off. He gazed at the gismo, then back at Ron. "That gismo didn't come off any old radio or television set. It didn't come from a telephone truck, either." His voice was low. "It came from that spaceship, XR!"

3

Is that you, XR?

Both boys were quiet for a moment; then Ron stood up. He stared at the crystal set and shook his head. "If that gismo fell from a spaceship, it would still be orbiting out there." He waved his arm toward the window.

"Not if the spaceship wasn't out there orbiting the earth, too," Jerry said.

"But if the gismo entered the earth's atmosphere, it would burn up! You know that." Ron exclaimed.

"Not if it was lost while the spaceship was in the atmosphere," Jerry suggested.

Ron shook his head. "It would be smashed to pieces when it hit the ground . . . like my transistor radio."

Jerry leaned forward. "Not if it fell off a spaceship that was *on* the ground."

Ron grinned. "Back of Gormley's shop? Ha!"

"Well, maybe they were investigating something."

"Like the trash boxes, maybe?"

"Who knows what they investigate when they land!" Jerry said. "We know they *do* land, and there was a UFO over Bridgeville the other night!"

Ron picked the headphones up and slipped them on. "I've got to hear this thing again to believe it!"

But before Ron had the earphones adjusted, a loud wail of music filled the room. Ron spread his hands and shook his head.

Jerry ran to the door and stuck his head into the hall. "Hey, Lou! Turn your record player down! We can't hear my radio in here."

"Turn your radio up, then," Lou yelled back.

"I can't. It's my crystal radio."

"Tough!" Lou shouted.

"Darn her! Just a minute, Ron, I'll be right back." Jerry started for the door, but Ron stopped him.

"Forget it, Jerry. Unhook the gismo and we'll take it over to my place. I've got my crystal radio set up in the workshop, where it's quiet."

Jerry removed the gismo from the wires and slid it into his jeans. Together the boys clattered down the stairs and out the back door. They slipped through the hole in the cyprus hedge that separated their two yards and ran across the grass to the workshop behind the Baily garage.

Inside the shop stood a long workbench under a row of windows. Ron pulled his crystal set out from behind a clutter of tools. "You attach the gismo while I check the aerial."

Carefully Jerry wired the gismo to Ron's crystal radio. He picked the earphones up and slipped them over his head. He could hear the hum of the gismo as he moved the tuner across the coil.

Ron came back. "We should have brought your earphones along, too."

Jerry started to take the headphones off. "I'll go back and get mine," he said.

Ron held his hand up. "No, don't bother. I've got an old telephone in this junk box, somewhere. We can hook that on and listen through the receiver." He bent over and rummaged about in a large box under the workbench. He pushed aside an old world globe, several broken plastic cars, and pulled a dusty old-fashioned standing telephone from the box.

Three wires of different colors, with spade clips on the ends, dangled from the telephone cord. Ron connected a checkered yellow-and-black wire and a brown wire across the capacitor of the crystal radio. The third wire, a checkered black-and-white one, hung free.

Ron jumped up and sat on the workbench. Placing the telephone beside him, he took the receiver from the hook and put it to his ear. The gismo hummed. "A okay," he signaled to Jerry.

There was a crackle of static and the familiar high-pitched voice broke in. "XR . . . calling XR . . . we lost your signal for a short while, but it's coming in loud and clear now. Please report back to Base Ship Plymo, if you are able. We repeat: if you are disabled, repair craft are waiting for you at crater 7 del 5, natural satellite, Planet Three, Sun G six zero eight, Syklo Galaxy . . . ."

Jerry glanced at Ron. "Base Ship Plymo . . . that must be where the message is coming from! I wonder where it is?"

"What I'm wondering is how come this guy is talking in our language. It doesn't figure." Ron scratched his head. "All that the radio astronomers have been able to pull in so far are funny squeaks and blips from outer space. They can't decode them yet, either. This still sounds phoney to me!"

"It isn't!" Jerry exclaimed. "Look, Ron, some spaceship named XR is in earth's atmosphere with its communication system knocked out and . . ." Jerry glanced at the gismo, fading back to pink, and snapped his fingers. *"Hey, wait a minute!"* He pointed at the gismo. "Do you suppose that could be . . ."

Ron leaned forward. "The communication system to a spaceship?" He shook his head. "It's too little."

"But, Ron, every time we hook the gismo up the little guy says 'we're beginning to receive your transmitting signal loud and clear.'"

The high voice cut in "XR . . . calling XR . . . we are waiting for your message . . . XR . . . calling XR . . ."

Ron shook his head again. "This is beginning to sound like an endless tape to me!" He was playing idly with the checkered black-and-white wire that hung free from the telephone cord. "XR . . ." Ron mimicked. "Spaceship XR, where are you?" Grinning, he slipped the spade clip of the black-and-white wire over the free knob of the gismo. He picked the telephone up and held it in front of him like a microphone. He lowered his voice until he sounded like a gruff policeman. "Look, Chief," he said into the telephone mouthpiece, "we're stuck down here on Planet Three in this crazy swamp."

Jerry laughed. He took the phone from Ron's hand and spoke into it. "Yeah, Chief, the sergeant, here, got to watching some majorettes practicing on the football field, and he ran smack into the swamp."

Ron grabbed the phone back from Jerry. "He's wrong, sir, it was the light from their batons that blinded me."

Jerry grinned and leaned over to the mouthpiece. "But don't worry, Chief, nobody's bothered us yet. We're pretending to be swamp gas."

Ron threw his head back and laughed. There was a loud crackle of static. The voice from the radio sounded eager. "Calling XR . . . We read you! A swamp, did you say? Would

you please repeat that message again . . . slowly
. . . over."

Ron was still chuckling. "Well, Chief,
we're . . ."

Jerry grabbed the phone from Ron's hand.
"Cut it, Ron!" His voice was sharp. He
slammed the receiver onto the hook.

Ron looked at Jerry. "What did you do
that for?"

Jerry's eyes grew rounder as he stared at
the phone.

Ron leaned forward. "What's the matter?"

Jerry swallowed and pointed at the phone.
"He heard us! That guy *heard* us!"

"So what if he did?"

"Don't you know who that is?"

Ron shrugged his shoulders. "Who else,
but some ham operator?"

Jerry's voice was tense. "For gosh sakes,
Ron, wise up! That's no ham operator. That
man's from *outer space!*"

4

Park Lane, Planet Three

Ron was quiet while Jerry's words sank in. He turned and grinned sheepishly at Jerry. "If he really is a man from outer space, I'll bet our message really shook him, huh?"

Jerry smiled too. "Yeah. Maybe we'd better call him back and tell him it was just a joke."

"You call him, Jerry, I don't know what to say to a spaceman."

"Well, neither do I, except tell him we've found the gismo."

Ron reached over and stroked the furry wires with his fingers. "You really think it's a communication system to a spaceship?"

"There's one way to find out," Jerry said and lifted the receiver on the telephone. "Calling Base Ship Plymo . . . calling Base Ship Plymo . . . over." Ron grabbed the earphones and put them over his head.

The static crackled and the high-pitched voice had relief in it. "We read you, XR, go ahead . . ."

Jerry hesitated. "I'm sorry, sir, about that swamp thing. It was just a joke. This isn't XR calling, this is . . . its communication system, I guess . . . what I mean is, I'm Jerry Cole, and I found this gismo, see, and hooked it up to a crystal radio, and that's how I'm talking with you."

"Jer—ry Cole?" The voice sounded puzzled. "Who are you?"

"Oh, I live here on earth . . . Planet Three, that is . . . you know, near Sun G six zero eight in Syklo Galaxy?"

"An . . . Earth—ling?" The voice sounded surprised.

"Yes, sir, I guess that's what you'd call me."

There was no sound from the receiver, and Jerry clicked it up and down. "Can you still hear me, sir?"

"Yes, yes . . . I can hear you. . . . An Earthling, you say. A scientist, no doubt."

"Well, not yet," Jerry said. "I'm in seventh grade . . . so is my friend here, Ron Baily . . . he's listening in, too."

"You . . . you are *children*?"

"Well, not exactly. What is your name, sir?"

There was a long pause as though the listener was thinking and suddenly became aware of the question. "Oh, I'm sorry! My name is Monaal. But why . . . how . . ."

Jerry grinned at Ron. "You mean how come I'm talking with you?"

Monaal hesitated again. "Yes . . . as you say . . . 'how come?' "

"Well, you see I found this gismo in the weeds and . . ."

"Gismo?"

"Yes, this little rectangular thing. It has knobs on three sides, tiny wires all over the top, and it glows red when you talk."

"Oh *that*!"

"So I hooked the gismo to my crystal radio set. I heard your message about XR and . . ."

Ron leaned over to the telephone mouthpiece. "I'm Ron, sir. When I hooked the telephone to the radio, you heard us!"

"Children! Mere children!" Monaal seemed to be talking to himself. "The culture on Planet Three is advancing!"

"Please, Mr. Monaal, could you tell us if this gismo is the communication system for your spacecraft XR?" Jerry asked.

"It's part of the system, yes. Just where did you find it?"

Jerry related his discovery of the gismo.

"Were there power lines close by?" Monaal asked.

"Oh, sure. They run all along the alley," Jerry answered.

"That might explain it." Monaal seemed to be talking to himself again.

"Explain what, sir?" Jerry asked.

"I'm afraid you wouldn't understand, Jerry. That is your name, isn't it?"

"Yes, sir, I'm Jerry."

"Now, Jerry, I'm going to ask you some questions, and I want you to answer them as carefully as you can." Monaal spoke slowly. He sounded like Miss Mills about to give a test.

"Where exactly on Planet Three—Earth, as you call it—are you located?"

Jerry looked at Ron. "Well, sir, that's pretty hard to do unless I'm looking at a map."

"Wait!" Ron jumped down from the workbench. "I've got this old globe here in the junk box. He rummaged under the workbench and brought the dusty globe of the world out. He dusted it clean with his shirttail, and set it on the workbench in front of Jerry.

Jerry turned the globe until the map of the United States faced him. "Mr. Monaal, I have a map now, can you hear me?"

"Yes, Jerry, I read you. Go ahead."

"Well, we're about halfway between the North Pole and the equator in North America —that's the continent with oceans on either side, a big bay at the top, and a big gulf at the bottom . . . some very large lakes up at the top right-hand corner. . . ."

Monaal's voice broke in, "And a large river running down the center?"

"Yes, the Mississippi River, but it's not quite in the center."

Monaal's voice had a smile in it. "Well, almost in the center. How near to this river are you, Jerry?"

"Not very near. We're about halfway between the Mississippi and the Atlantic ocean . . . that's the ocean on the right-hand side of the continent."

Ron leaned over. "But we are near a river, sir. We're in a V right between two big ones, the Wabash and the Ohio, in southern Indiana."

Jerry turned. "Look, Ron, he wouldn't know the names of the rivers, and state lines don't show from the air." He turned to the mouthpiece. "We're halfway between the tip of Lake Michigan—that's the big lake farthest down in the continent—and the Gulf of Mexico—that's the gulf at the bottom of the continent."

"Oh, yes! I've found the place where the two rivers come together," Monaal exclaimed.

"Do you have a map, sir?" Jerry asked.

"Yes, an exploratory type, but it isn't named like yours." Monaal answered. "Now, Jerry, locate your town for me."

Carefully Jerry described Bridgeville's position between the two rivers. "And Park Lane is where we live. Our houses are right across the street from the park. Ron's is a big white house with a green roof, and mine is the yellow one next door with a white roof."

"Are you in one of those houses right now?" Monaal asked.

"No, we're out in Ron's workshop back of his garage."

"You've done very well in locating yourselves," Monaal said.

Ron leaned over. "Are there really spacecraft flying around our Earth, Mr. Monaal?"

"Why, of course," Monaal said. "Lots of spacecraft!"

"What do they look like?" Ron was eager. "Are they like saucers or cigars or eggs or tops?"

"Saucers? Cigars? I'm afraid I don't know what you're talking about." Monaal sounded puzzled.

"I mean, are the spacecraft round and flat shaped, or long and thin?"

"Well, that depends." Monaal said. "We have many kinds, but the ones from our galaxy that enter Planet Three's atmosphere are usually cylindrical base ships that house the dome-topped explorer discs."

"How big are the explorers?" Jerry asked.

"Oh, many sizes. Some are perhaps eighty feet across, some nearer thirty feet, while some unmanned ones are very small. But you'll have a chance to see one soon, if the description of your location is accurate."

"When?" Jerry and Ron spoke at once.

"When your continent has turned away from your sun and is halfway through the darkness."

"You mean, tonight?" Ron asked.

"Yes, tonight . . . I must sign off now . . ."

"Wait, Mr. Monaal, wait! How did you learn our language?" Jerry asked, but it was too late. The voice had clicked off. The gismo was fading back to pink. All that was left was a faint hum.

5

Spaceship at Midnight

Slowly, Jerry put the telephone receiver back on the hook and began to unwind the wires on the gismo. He grinned at Ron, who was lifting the earphones from his head. "*Now* do you believe me?"

Ron grinned back and laid the headset by the crystal radio. "What do you think! Spaceships tonight! Wow!" He gave the globe a whirl. "'When your continent is halfway through darkness,' that's midnight, right?"

"Right!" Jerry slipped the gismo into his

jeans pocket. "Think you can stay awake that long?"

"Are you kidding?" Ron jumped down from the workbench. "I'd stay awake for a week to see a real spaceship!"

"Me, too." Jerry followed Ron out of the shop.

Ron turned. "Hey, tomorrow's Saturday. Bring your sleeping bag over, and we'll camp out here in the yard tonight. That way we can watch for the spaceship together."

"Neat idea!" Jerry exclaimed. "I'll bring my pup tent."

"Okay, but we're sleeping with our heads outside so we can watch the sky. Man! Real spaceships! I can hardly wait. Let's set the tent up right now."

"I'll have to ask Mom." Jerry started for the hole in the hedge.

"Listen, Jerry, don't mention why we want to sleep out. She might not understand. You know how parents are."

"Sure, I know." Jerry smiled back and disappeared through the hedge.

He was back soon, the rolled pup tent balanced on his head. He dropped it on the ground. "Mom says it's okay. Where shall we set the tent up?"

Ron strolled over to a spot near the center of the back lawn. With his hands in his hip pockets, he squinted up at the sky. "How about here? No trees in the way."

Jerry joined Ron and squinted up, too. He lifted his hands, spread them out flat, side by side, circled them around his head, and zoomed them down to flutter in front of him like a hovering saucer. "Okay, spaceship right here, midnight!"

It was growing dusk when they crawled into the pup tent. "I brought along some eats." Jerry pulled an apple from each jean pocket.

"Me, too." Ron held up a box of Whacky Snacks.

Jerry peeled his jeans off and climbed into his sleeping bag. "Mom wanted to know why I was going to bed so early," he said.

Ron grinned. "What did you tell her?"

"I said I was tired."

"Did she buy that?"

"Nope, so I told her you and I had lots of things to discuss."

"Yeah, well, grown-ups don't understand you got to adjust to things a lot when you sleep outside, like this air mattress, for instance. Here, hold my flashlight, Jerry, while I blow this sack up some more."

46

Jerry held the flashlight and listened to the air wheeze through the air mattress tubes as Ron blew into it. "Wonder what my mom and dad would say if I'd told them we were going to see a real live spaceship tonight."

Ron flipped his thumb over the air mattress valve and screwed the valve shut. "They'd have thought you were kidding."

"Yeah. They'd probably say 'watch out, don't get too close,' like they were going along with a gag."

Ron snaked down into his sleeping bag and pulled the zipper up. "Sure, grown-ups are all alike. They think we're always making things up just to get their attention, or something."

The two boys lay with their heads outside the tent. Crickets chirped in the grass. Far in the distance they could hear the drone of the city street sweeper on its nightly trip around Bridgeville. The stars were beginning to prick through the dark blue above. Jerry put his hands under his head and gazed up at the twinkling lights.

"Where do you suppose he lives? Monaal, I mean," Jerry said.

"Maybe on Mars or Venus," Ron suggested.

"I don't think so."

"Why not?"

"Because if he did, he wouldn't be talking about his galaxy and our galaxy."

"But other galaxies are too far away," Ron said. "Why, it would take a million years for spaceships to come from the nearest galaxy to ours."

"Maybe they don't have the same length years we do. Maybe they've figured out how to live as long as they want to."

Ron rolled over and leaned on his elbow. "But what kind of metal would they use for spaceships that could travel for a million years?"

"Probably some sort of metal we don't even know about. Gases on their planet could be different. Gravity could be different. Everything could be different."

"Yeah," Ron nodded. "Even the people could be different. . . . Two heads, four arms, six feet."

"Not too much different, Ron. They talk like we do. Monaal did anyway."

"That still bugs me," Ron shook his head. "How does he know our language?"

"Maybe they've studied our radio and television signals that are bouncing off our space satellites. If they're advanced enough to build spaceships that travel from one galaxy to another, they're sharp enough to decode our signals."

"But why would they learn to talk our language? What are they up to? Man! I've got a lot of questions to ask Monaal!" Ron reached for the Whacky Snacks box and set it between them.

"Me, too," Jerry sighed and tossed a handful of Whacky Snacks into his mouth.

It was near midnight when Jerry sat up and felt inside his sleeping bag. Ron, heavy-lidded, lay on his back. "What you fussing around for?"

"Oh, a bunch of Whacky Snacks got in here somehow."

"Yeah, I feel a couple in my sack, too, but I'm too tired to look for them. I'm beginning to think Monaal's forgotten all about us. Isn't it about morning?"

Jerry glanced toward the east. "It isn't getting light yet."

Ron rolled over on his side. "I'm going to sleep. Wake me up if anything happens."

"Okay," Jerry threw a Whacky Snack onto the grass and burrowed into his sleeping bag. He turned over and was plumping his pillow when he caught the motion of light toward the north. He sat up. A wedge of tiny stars seemed to be moving across the sky. They grew into globes of light. When they were directly overhead, the leading light glided away from the group and fluttered down like a leaf, growing larger and larger.

Jerry reached over and shook Ron. "Wake up! It's here, Ron, it's here!"

Ron rose sleepily on one elbow. "What's here?"

"The spaceship, stupid! Look!" He pointed at the globe of light which had grown to the size of a large platter. It hovered over the park.

Ron, wide awake now, sat up in his sleeping bag. The glowing disc tilted to one side and glided silently toward the yard. Its brightness faded somewhat, and Jerry could clearly see a wide circle of red and white lights revolving underneath the rim. The spaceship drew nearer and nearer until it blotted out the sky. The crickets had stopped chirping. Jerry was aware of a strange buzzing sound that seemed to come from directly above his forehead. The great spaceship floated over the yard until it reached the garage. There it bobbed not ten feet from the roof with a high, soft whining sound.

Jerry could see the red and white revolving

lights reflected on the concave metal surface beneath, where a hatch was sliding open directly in the center. From the brightly lighted interior of the ship, a silver-colored metal wand began to descend slowly.

Jerry and Ron both gasped. On a small platform at the bottom of the wand, stood a little man dressed in a glinting metallic suit.

6

Anyone home?

Jerry and Ron stared in amazement. The wand from the spaceship touched the roof of the garage, and the spaceman, no taller than Jerry or Ron, stepped onto the ridgepole. He stood for a moment looking down. The red and white lights revolving above him glinted in his round bubble helmet. Their reflection made him seem faceless. A small square box, with a blue light blinking from it, was strapped to his chest. His metallic one-piece suit fitted him like a skin diver's wet suit. His shoes were large and awkward looking. Slowly, the spaceman shuffled to the edge of the roof. Hesitating a moment, he bent his knees and jumped. He floated down to the ground like a maple leaf.

He paused and looked about him, then bent his bubble helmet forward as though he were looking at the box on his chest. He turned slowly. When the blue light blinked directly at the pup tent he stopped moving. Jerry and Ron froze. The spaceman hesitated a moment, then swung around and shuffled toward the workshop. The boys could see him fumble with the knob, push on the door, and go inside.

"What does he want in there?" Ron whispered.

"Don't you remember? That's where we talked to Monaal this afternoon."

"Yeah! I bet he thinks we're still in there," Ron whispered.

"I bet he wants to talk to us some more," Jerry said. He began to climb out of his sleeping bag. "I'm going in there."

"Maybe it isn't safe," Ron whispered. "He might shoot you with a ray gun, or he might be radioactive, or something."

"Are you crazy? He won't hurt me—he knows I'm his friend. Besides, if it's Monaal, I want to ask some more questions."

"Hey, yeah! Me too!" Ron struggled from his sleeping bag. "I'll go with you."

Jerry reached for his jeans. They felt clammy as he stuck his feet into them. He stood up. No time for socks and sneakers. Through the workshop windows, he could see the blue light bobbing about. The spaceman must have climbed onto the workbench, he thought.

Suddenly Jerry felt very awkward. How would he greet the spaceman? What would he say? He was glad Ron would be with him. He glanced down. "Come on, Ron, what's holding you up?"

"These jeans! They're wrong side out."

"Put them on anyway."

Ron snorted. "Ever try to zip a pair wrong side out?" He rose to his knees, and heaved to his feet. "Okay, let's go."

Quickly the boys approached the workshop. The wet grass licked at their bare feet. They had just reached the corner of the building when the blue light blinked at them from the workshop doorway.

"Hi," Jerry's voice sounded very loud in the quiet night.

The spaceman started, then ran clumsily away from the shop.

"Hey, wait! We won't hurt you." Jerry ran after him.

The little man bent forward, touched his boots, and instantly rose into the air. By the time the boys reached the spot where he had been, the spaceman had floated to the garage roof. They could hear his feet patter across the shingles.

Jerry ran backward until he could see the rooftop. "Please, don't go away, please!" He called up.

"We won't hurt you, honest!" Ron chimed in. "Look, we only want to ask you some questions."

By now the spaceman had reached the silver wand. The boys heard him rap sharply on it. Quickly the wand retracted into the ship and carried the spaceman with it. The hatch slid shut. The barely audible whine increased while the red and white lights whirred faster. With a rush of air that swayed the top of the maple tree in Jerry's yard, the spaceship shot upward into the night.

The boys stood in the wet grass and

watched the spaceship diminish to a globe of light high above. It joined the waiting wedge of lights that wheeled like a flock of pigeons and streaked northward out of sight.

A window slid up. "Ron?" It was his mother's voice, low and concerned. "Are you two all right?"

"S—sure, we're fine."

"What were you shouting about?"

"Ah, it was nothing, Mom."

"Then please quiet down, or you'll wake the whole neighborhood."

"Okay, Mom."

The boys shuffled toward the tent. Jerry hunched his shoulders and put his hands in his pockets. "Should we tell our folks what happened tonight?"

Ron shook his head. "Not yet. They wouldn't understand."

The boys sat down on their sleeping bags and climbed out of their jeans again. Ron wiped his wet feet with a leg of his jeans. "I still can't figure out why Monaal told us the spaceship was coming and then wouldn't talk with us . . . just ran away."

Jerry rubbed his feet against the pup tent. "Maybe that wasn't Monaal. Maybe it was some other guy he sent."

"But what did he want in the workshop?"

Jerry inched into his sleeping bag. "I told you—that's where we were when we talked with Monaal this afternoon. Remember?"

Ron pulled up the zipper on his sleeping bag. "But if he thought we'd be in the shop, he must have wanted to see us about something."

"Sure, he probably did."

"Then why did he run away?"

Jerry sank onto his pillow. "I guess I scared him when I ran after him."

Ron put his hands under the back of his head and looked up at the stars. "Man, it's weird! What did that spaceship come all the way down here for?"

The boys were silent. The crickets began to chirp again. Jerry could hear the street sweeper droning down Park Lane. Why *had* the spaceship come down, he wondered. Suddenly he felt a cold chill run through him. He sat up and reached for his jeans. He felt in the pockets. Thank goodness, it was still there. Slowly he drew the tiny metal object out and held it in his hand. He leaned over. "Ron?"

"Yeah?"

"I bet I know why they came down."

"Why?"

"To get the gismo!"

It wasn't until the next afternoon, following Saturday-morning lawn mowing, that Jerry and Ron stepped into the workshop.

"Hey look!" Ron pointed at the workbench. The telephone lay on its side, the stand and mouthpiece removed. The receiver, too, had been taken apart.

Jerry snapped his fingers. "The spaceman! Remember, we could see his blue light blinking through the window like he was doing something on the workbench?"

"Yeah!" Ron fastened the base back onto the telephone and screwed the mouthpiece in place. "Why would he want to wreck it like this?"

"To get at the gismo, stupid! He thought it was inside the telephone."

Ron fastened the telephone to the crystal radio and checked the aerial and ground. He rubbed his hands together. "Okay, let's have the gismo."

Jerry reached into his pockets. He felt first in one pocket, then in the other, but his fingers touched no slippery metal. He looked at Ron in dismay. "It's gone! The gismo is gone!"

7

Gismo, Gismo, who has the Gismo?

Hastily Jerry felt in his hip pockets, then in his side pockets, but no gismo.

"Maybe it fell into your sleeping bag last night," Ron suggested.

"No, had it this morning. I remember I put it right in here." Jerry slapped his right thigh.

"Got any holes?"

Jerry ran his hands inside his pockets again. "Nope."

"Hey, I know!" Ron exclaimed. "It fell out while you were mowing your lawn."

"Yeah! Let's go look." Jerry ran out of the workshop with Ron after him. The boys dropped to their hands and knees and crawled about on the grass. At last Jerry spied the gismo nearly hidden in a grass clump by the fence. He pounced on it. "Here it is!"

He was brushing the grass clippings from its tiny wires on top when his mother called to him from the back door. "Jerry, may I see you for a minute?"

Jerry shoved the gismo into his pants pocket and scuffed to the steps.

"Here." His mother slipped some money into his shirt pocket. "Run down to Bob's Barber Shop and get yourself a haircut." She reached out and rumpled his red thatch. "You're beginning to look like a troll!"

"Okay, I'll do it later." Jerry turned.

"No, Jerry, not later—*now!*"

"Why not later?"

"Because Bob closes his shop early Saturday afternoons, remember?"

"Aw gee!"

"And please change your jeans. I won't have you running around town with grass-stained knees. Come on, into the house now, chop chop." His mother held the back door open.

Jerry glanced over his shoulder at Ron and sighed heavily. "Guess I'll have to see you later."

Ron ran his fingers through his shaggy hair. "I'll ride down with you. My mom says I need a haircut, too."

Jerry ran up to his room, climbed out of his jeans and into a clean pair. He hurried down the stairs and out the back door. Ron was on his bike cruising back and forth over Dodie's hopscotch. Jerry hopped onto his bike and together they headed for town. They parked their bikes outside the barbershop.

Inside, Jerry and Ron slouched into chairs to wait their turn. Clippers hummed and scissors snipped while they thumbed through the magazines.

Ron jabbed Jerry in the ribs with his elbow. "Hey, look!" He held a picture of a reported UFO sighting. "How about that!"

Jerry took the magazine. "Yeah!" He studied the picture carefully. "That looks just like the one last night. Maybe it's XR."

"Next!" Bob beckoned a pudgy finger at Jerry.

Jerry walked to the barber chair still reading the article.

"What's grabbing you there, son?" Bob asked. He flicked the towel around Jerry's shoulders.

"This article about UFO's." Jerry held the magazine up. "You read it yet?"

Bob clicked his scissors. "Sure, I read all that stuff." He ran a comb through Jerry's hair. "If you ask me, I think it's all a big hoax."

"Don't you believe in ships from outer space?" Jerry winked at Ron.

Bob snipped busily at the top of Jerry's head. "Who does? There's logical explanations for everything we see, son. Maybe those things are lights from airplanes. Maybe they're beacons reflecting on flat clouds. They could even be experimental aircraft from our own country or some other government. From outer space? That's impossible!"

"But if we can figure out spacecraft that fly to the moon," Jerry said, "why can't people from other planets figure out spacecraft that fly from their planet to ours?"

Bob laughed above the hum of clippers. "With little men inside of them, I suppose? You kids and your imaginations!"

Jerry and Ron pedaled home, their heads smelling strongly of cheap cologne. Ron grinned across at Jerry. "I wonder what Bob would have said if we'd told him about last night?"

Jerry shook his head. "No grown-up would ever believe us!"

"Yeah," Ron agreed. "Have I got questions to ask Monaal! Wow! Come on, I'll race you home."

The boys pedaled furiously down Park Lane and up Jerry's driveway. Ron won. Jerry leaned his bike against the maple tree and followed Ron through the hole in the hedge. The two went inside the workshop.

Ron held his hand out. "Okay, the gismo."

Jerry reached into his pockets. "Oh, no! I left it in my other jeans! Be right back." He sprinted out the door and through the hedge, banged into the house, and took the stairs two at a time. He puffed into his room, but no jeans lay by the bed where he had dropped them. He ran to the closet. His mother hadn't hung them up, either. He clattered downstairs again. "Mom," he called loudly, "what happened to the jeans I took off?"

His mother came into the hall with an armload of clothes. "They're in the washing machine, why?"

"Oh, no!" Jerry exclaimed. "Did you find the gismo in one of the pockets?"

"The gismo?" his mother asked. "Oh, you mean that little silver brush thing?"

"Yeah, that's it. Where is it?" Jerry asked eagerly.

"I put it on the windowsill on the back porch."

"Thank gosh!" Jerry ran to the back porch, but only a bottle of detergent sat on the windowsill. "It isn't here, Mom!" he wailed.

"Well, someone may have picked it up. Ask Dad, he's in the basement. Ask Lou, or Dodie. They might have seen it."

Jerry hurried down the basement steps two at a time. His father was gluing a rung onto a chair. "Dad, did you by any chance take my gismo off the windowsill on the back porch?"

"Your gismo?"

"Yeah, you know—that metal thing I showed you the other night?"

His father shook his head. "No, I didn't."

Jerry rushed up the basement steps, then to the bedrooms upstairs. He leaned panting against Lou's door jam. "You got my gismo, Lou?"

65

Lou looked up from a magazine. "Your what?"

"My gismo—that metal thing on the windowsill on the back porch."

"You're out of your tree!"

"Have you got it?"

"No!"

Jerry swung around and into Dodie's room, but she wasn't there. He ran downstairs again. "Mom, is Dodie here?"

"I think she's outside somewhere," his mother answered.

Jerry ran to the back door. Dodie was playing hopscotch on the asphalt in front of the garage. He slammed out the back door. "Dodie, did you take anything off the windowsill on the back porch?" he asked.

She turned and looked at him innocently. "What thing?"

"My gismo."

"What would I want with an old gismo, whatever *that* is!" Dodie turned back and carefully threw her lager.

Jerry watched it hit the asphalt with a clink and slide into the last square. Then he gasped in horror. There lay his gismo!

8

Orders from Monaal

Jerry bent down and scooped the gismo up from the hopscotch square. He shook it in Dodie's face. "Look! *This* is the gismo! And if you've wrecked it, you'll be sorry!" He turned and ran toward the hole in the hedge.

"Mother—r—r!" Dodie wailed, "Jerry has my lager!"

Ron met Jerry in the shop doorway. "What took you so long?"

Jerry wiped his hand across his forehead.

"Man! What I've been through! You wouldn't believe it! But here's the gismo. I hope it's okay."

Quickly he attached it to the crystal radio. Ron slipped the earphones over his head, and Jerry put the telephone receiver to his ear. They listened anxiously for the gismo's hum. It was very faint at first, but gradually grew louder and louder.

Jerry cleared his throat. "This is Jerry Cole calling Base Ship Plymo. . . . Jerry Cole calling Base Ship Plymo . . ."

There was a sputter of static. "This is Base Ship Plymo, go ahead, please."

"Is this Mr. Monaal?"

"Yes it is, Jerry."

"Sir, we saw the spaceship last night, like you promised we would."

"Yes, I know. You gave us very good directions, Jerry."

"Then it was you who went into the workshop!"

"No, that was one of my men."

"Why did he run away? Didn't you tell him we were his friends?"

"All our men are cautioned not to make contact with inhabitants of other planets, if

68

they are not prepared. He wasn't expecting to see you."

"Then what did he come down for?"

"I think you know the answer to that, Jerry."

"The gismo?"

"Yes."

"But why do you need it back? Couldn't you repair XR with another communication system just like this one?"

"It's a rather important piece of equipment, Jerry. I hope you realize that."

"Oh, yes, sir, I do. But don't you have others you could use? I'd like to keep this gismo, if you don't mind."

"No, Jerry, I'm sorry."

"You mean this is the only one you've got?"

Monaal's voice was earnest. "Can I trust you, Jerry?"

"Sure, Mr. Monaal, sure!"

"Then tonight at midnight bring the gismo to the park."

"Couldn't I keep it just a little while longer, please? If it had fallen in the ocean or on a snowy mountain somewhere, you wouldn't have found it. In fact, you'd never have known where it was at all if Ron and I hadn't hooked it up and told you."

"I know that, Jerry, and I'm grateful to you."

Ron leaned over and spoke into the mouthpiece. "We'd take real good care of it. You see, we've got lots of questions we want to ask you."

"I'm sure you have! I'll see you in the park tonight." Monaal spoke slowly. "Midnight, remember, *with the gismo*. And will you promise me something else?"

"Yes, sir," both boys answered at once.

"Just the two of you."

Jerry sighed. "Yes, sir, just Ron and me. We'll be there. But Mr. Monaal, won't you answer one question now, please?"

Ron leaned over to the mouthpiece quickly. "Yes, sir, please tell us how you learned to speak our language?"

But even as Ron spoke there was a sputter of static, followed by a final click, and the gismo faded from cherry red to faint pink.

Slowly Jerry put the receiver back on the telephone. "He didn't answer us again. Man! I wish I knew why he's got to have the gismo back!"

Ron took the earphones off and laid them

on the workbench. "He said it was an important piece of equipment, that's why."

"Sure, I know that! But if they've got lots of spacecraft cruising around this planet, like he said, and they all have communication systems, they must have replacements somewhere."

Ron put his chin in his hands. "Maybe the gismos are all back at home base. Maybe they don't have any around here."

"Look, he said repair craft were waiting for XR on the moon, didn't he? Well, they must have some spare parts on the moon."

Ron grinned. "Maybe they're fresh out of gismos up there, too."

"Oh, sure!" Jerry scoffed. "You know something else? He really didn't tell us anything except to meet him tonight and give the gismo back. We'd better sleep outside again tonight."

Ron yawned. "I guess so, but let's take an alarm clock with us and set it for eleven-thirty. I know I won't be able to stay awake that long."

"Okay." Jerry unfastened the gismo from the crystal radio and held it in his hand. "I guess I'd better guard this with my life, huh?"

Ron held his hand out. "Maybe *I* should hang onto it—you might lose it again."

"Don't worry. I won't lose it. I'm hanging

onto this gismo until I see Monaal tonight. And he's not getting it back until he answers a few questions first!"

"That's telling him!" Ron laughed.

That night at supper when Jerry announced he was going to sleep outside, his mother shook her head. "No, Jerry, one night of no sleep is enough."

"I slept last night!" Jerry said indignantly.

"A little, perhaps." His mother smiled. "But those circles under your eyes give you away."

"Please, Mom, I've *got* to sleep outside tonight."

Dodie reached for a slice of bread. "Why?"

"It's none of your business why!" Jerry stabbed at his meat loaf with a fork.

"Jerry," his father said, "watch yourself!" He passed the butter to Dodie. "I'm interested too, Son. Just why must you sleep outside tonight?"

Jerry ducked his head and swallowed a big mouthful of food. "Well, Ron and I . . . we . . . just *like* to, that's all. And there's no school tomorrow."

"That doesn't sound like a very urgent

reason," his father said. "Your mother's right —you'd better sleep in your own bed tonight. Those circles under your eyes are pretty fierce."

"Oh, Dad!"

"You heard me, Jerry!"

After supper Jerry phoned Ron. "Listen, Ron, I've got a little problem here—my folks. They won't let me sleep outside tonight."

"Yeah? Well, you're not the only one," Ron answered. Mom says we were too noisy last night. I can't sleep outside either."

"What are we going to do?"

"I guess we'll just have to set our alarm clocks and sneak out at eleven-thirty," Ron suggested.

"Yeah? I guess so, but it's going to be pretty hard here. Dad and Mom usually watch a late movie on TV Saturday nights."

"Maybe you can sneak out the back way between commercials. They won't be wandering around the house then."

"Yeah, I'll try," Jerry said. "Meet you at the hedge at eleven-forty-five, okay?"

"Okay." Ron hung up.

When Jerry went to bed, he set his alarm and put it under the corner of his pillow. If it buzzed too loudly someone would come into his room to see what was up. But it was hard going to sleep with the hum of an electric clock so close to his ear.

Jerry lay thinking about Monaal. What would he look like, he wondered. He would be small like the other spaceman, Jerry felt sure. But what would his face look like? He hadn't been able to see any features of the man the night before. The revolving lights from the spaceship had reflected too brightly on the helmet surface for that. Jerry closed his eyes and let the happenings of the night before slide across his mind. The great floating spaceship . . . the silver wand . . . the spaceman . . . the strange buzzing sound over his forehead . . . the sound wouldn't stop. It grew louder and louder.

Jerry opened his eyes with a start. The buzzing wasn't over his forehead, it was under his pillow. Quickly he turned the alarm clock off and peered closely at it. Yes, it was eleven-thirty. He swung his feet out of bed. Half an hour and Monaal would be back for the gismo.

9

The trouble with sisters

Jerry dressed quickly and patted his jeans pocket to make sure the gismo was in there. He pulled on his windbreaker and zipped it up. Quietly he opened his bedroom door. He could hear someone singing loudly on the television in the living room below. The lights in the downstairs hall were out. If he was quiet enough, he could slip through the hall to the kitchen without anyone in the living room hearing him. Jerry was stepping on the top step when he heard the front door bang shut. Lou had just come in from visiting Linda. She called into the living room, then came running up stairs. Jerry backed into his room. As he did so, his heel hit the bottom of the door and it banged against the wall.

Lou switched the upstairs hall light on. "Where do you think you're going?" she asked.

"Sh—h—h!" Jerry held his finger to his lips. "Not so loud. Do you want to wake Dodie up?"

Lou put her hands in the pockets of her slacks. "No, I want to know where you're sneaking off to at this hour, that's all."

"Well it's none of your business, see?" Jerry reached over and snapped off the hall light.

Lou snapped it on again. "Yes, it is my business!"

"Leave me alone, will you?" Jerry reached for the light switch again, but Lou grabbed his arm and twisted it around. Caught off-balance, Jerry went down on his knees. Lou quickly pushed him over onto his stomach and sat down on his back.

The scuffling woke Dodie, and she came out into the hall in her pajamas, rubbing her eyes. "What you fighting for?" she asked sleepily.

"Now see what you've done?" Jerry hissed from the floor. "You woke Dodie up!"

"I woke her up! You're the one that's trying to sneak out!" Lou exclaimed. "Here, Dodie, sit on his legs."

Jerry struggled to push Lou away, but Dodie obligingly plopped herself down on Jerry's legs, and he was pinned to the floor.

Lou folded her arms across her chest. "Okay, Jerry, where were you going?"

"Let me up, you dumb girls!" Jerry fumed.

"Not until you tell us," Lou said.

"Yeah, not till you tell us," Dodie echoed.

"Look, you two, I've got to be in the park in a few minutes. It's very, very important! Now will you quit being funny and get off?"

"Why do you have to be in the park?" Lou asked.

"Yeah, why?" Dodie echoed again.

"I've got to meet somebody, that's why! Let me up, please?"

"Who is it?" Lou insisted.

"Nobody you know!"

"Do I know him?" Dodie asked.

"No!" Jerry struggled to dislodge the girls, but they sat firm.

"Okay, I'll tell you. I've got to meet Monaal."

"Who's he?"

"A guy I know."

"Where's he from?"

"You wouldn't believe me if I told you!"

"Go ahead, try me." Lou said.

"Okay, he's from a spaceship."

"That's using your imagination!" Lou grinned.

"No, honest! Probably he's out there waiting for me in the park right now. Go ahead, see for yourself."

"And let you up?" Lou exclaimed. "I'm not that dumb!"

"Don't believe me, then, but the spaceship's there, I know it is!"

Lou turned. "Dodie, you go look out Jerry's window and see if there's a spaceship over the park."

"Okay." Dodie got up and ran into Jerry's room and over to the window.

"It's there, isn't it!" Jerry said.

"No," Dodie answered.

"Ha!" Lou exclaimed. "I knew it was another one of your tricks!"

"There's just a lot of little red and white lights going around in a circle up in the air," Dodie continued.

"That's it!" Jerry exclaimed. "That's the spaceship! Oh, *please* let me up, Lou, *please!*"

The earnestness in Jerry's voice was unmistakable, so Lou stood up. Jerry scrambled to his feet and ran into his room. Lou followed him to the window. The three of them stood looking out at the great spaceship that hovered in the dark sky above the park. The red and white lights rotating slowly under the rim reflected dimly onto the leaves of the treetops below.

"*Now* do you believe me?" Jerry cried. "I've got to meet Monaal. He's waiting for me over there."

"But why?" Lou asked.

"I'll tell you later. I haven't time now." Jerry started for the door.

"Jerry, wait!" There was concern in Lou's voice. "Is it safe to go out there?"

"Sure it's safe. Last night the spaceship went right over us. That's why I wanted to sleep outside again tonight." Jerry stopped at the doorway. "Listen, don't tell anyone about this spaceship, promise, Lou?"

"Okay."

"Promise, Dodie?"

"I promise."

Jerry reached out to turn the hall light out when his father called up the stairs. "Is everything all right up there, Lou?"

Jerry beckoned frantically to his sister.

Lou hurried to the door and stuck her head out. "Everything's okay, Daddy."

Dodie came padding toward the door. "Hey, Daddy, guess what? There's a spa—" she began, but Jerry cupped his hand over her mouth and held her struggling against him.

"Sh—h—h!" he hissed into her ear. "You promised not to tell!"

"Do I hear Dodie? Is she still awake up there?" Mr. Cole called.

"Oh, no," Lou said hastily. "She's just talking in her sleep."

"Well, turn the light out, Lou, and try to be a little quieter or you will wake her up. Good night."

"Good night, Daddy." Lou reached over and turned out the hall light.

"Thanks, pal," Jerry whispered. He released Dodie and peered down the stairs, then drew back. "Darn! He's in the kitchen now. I can't get out."

"Why don't you go through your window and down the maple tree?" Lou suggested.

"Yeah, I guess I'll have to." Jerry ran to the window and raised it softly. He unhooked the screen and straddled the window ledge. The gentle slope of the front porch roof was only a

few feet below. Quietly he eased himself out onto the shingles and crept toward the maple tree branch that curved over the porch. He climbed onto it and shinnied toward the trunk. Lou and Dodie stood with their heads out the window watching him. He lowered himself from branch to branch and jumped lightly to the ground.

He turned to run toward the park. In the gloom, he didn't see his bike. Down he went in a clatter of foot pedals and handlebar, his right foot turning under him. Sharp pain stabbed through his ankle.

Soon the front door squeaked open, and he could hear his father's footsteps on the front porch coming toward him. Quickly Jerry crawled behind the tree and held his breath. His father peered over the porch railing at the bike lying on the grass, then turned.

"It was just Jerry's bike that fell over, Alice," his father said. "That boy has got to learn to put his things away!" The front door squeaked shut again.

Jerry looked toward the hole in the hedge. Ron wasn't there. Was he over in the park, or had he overslept, Jerry wondered. It didn't matter. What mattered now was getting the gismo to the park.

Jerry pulled himself up and tried to step on his right foot, but it wouldn't hold him and he fell again. He looked toward the park. He had promised Monaal he'd be there at twelve. How could he keep his promise?

10

To the park by sister power

Jerry sat on the ground at the foot of the maple tree and leaned forward. He closed his eyes and rubbed his ankle. Tears of pain and anger squeezed out from under his eyelids. How could he have been so clumsy! He couldn't go to the park by himself.

He couldn't climb back up the tree. If he went in the house by the front or back door, he'd have to hop on one foot, and his parents would be sure to hear him. There would be all kinds of explaining to do. And they probably wouldn't believe a thing he told them about the gismo, the spaceship, and Monaal. He was really in a mess now!

"*Psst*, Jerry!" It was Lou. She was peering down at him from the edge of the porch roof. "What happened?" she whispered.

"I ran into my dumb bike and turned my ankle!" Jerry whispered back. "I can't stand on it. Lou, you've got to help me!"

"Okay, but how?"

Jerry thought a minute. "If I could hang onto someone I think I could make it over to the park."

"Hi!" Dodie's round face appeared beside Lou.

Lou turned. "Go back, Dodie!" she whispered. "You're in your pajamas! It's too cold out here for you."

"No it's not. I've got my bathrobe on, see?" Dodie stood up to show Lou.

Her older sister pulled her down quickly. "Don't stand on the edge of the roof like that! You'll fall off!"

"What's Jerry sitting there for?" Dodie whispered.

"He's hurt his ankle," Lou said. "Now keep quiet or they'll hear us downstairs." Lou looked over the edge of the roof. "Listen, Jerry," she whispered, "I'll come down, and you can hang onto me."

"How're you going to get down here?"

"The same way you did. I haven't forgotten how to climb down a tree."

"Okay, but be real quiet," Jerry warned.

Lou slung her leg over the branch and inched along till she reached the tree trunk. Slowly she lowered herself branch by branch till she could jump to the ground.

"I'm coming, too." Dodie was halfway down the maple before Jerry noticed her. "Oh, Dodie, go back!" Jerry whispered in exasperation.

Dodie dangled by her arms from the lowest branch, her feet still a long way from the ground. "Catch me, Lou."

"I thought I told you to go back!" Lou reached up and helped her sister to the ground.

"I want to help, too," Dodie whimpered.

"Well, just keep quiet, then," Jerry pleaded.

Lou extended her hand toward him. "Here, Jerry, grab hold." Jerry heaved himself to his good foot. Lou put her arm around him, and he put his arm over her shoulder. "Now, can you hop okay?" Lou asked.

Jerry hopped a step. "Yeah, I can make it."

Dodie walked around to his other side and put her arm around him. "You can lean on me, too," she whispered.

Jerry put his hand on Dodie's shoulder and, with a sister on either side, hopped down the driveway and across the street.

Their footsteps echoed through the empty park. Crickets chirped in the grass. Off in the distance Jerry could hear the drone of the street sweeper coming down Park Street. Jerry looked up. Through the treetops he could see the red and white lights of the spaceship wink on and off, as it circled slowly above the park.

"Where are you supposed to meet this spaceman?" Lou asked.

"He didn't say where . . . just come to the park," Jerry answered.

"How did you talk to him?" Lou asked.

"Remember that gismo I found?"

"That thing that looks like a mouse?" Lou exclaimed.

"My hopscotch lager?" Dodie asked.

"Stupid girls!" Jerry muttered.

Lou drew her arm away. "Okay, Jerry Cole, if we're so stupid, you can go the rest of the way alone. We just asked a couple of simple questions. Come on, Dodie."

Jerry grabbed Lou's arm. "Don't go! I'm sorry, I didn't mean that—it just slipped out. The gismo . . . it's a communication system from a spaceship."

Lou took hold of him again. "How did you find out?"

"I hooked it up to my crystal radio and Ron hooked on his telephone and we got this guy, Monaal. He told us what the gismo was and said he wanted it back. We saw the spaceship last night, but the spaceman Monaal sent down got scared, or something, and we didn't get to talk to him. Monaal's coming tonight, and, man! have I got questions to ask him!"

They had reached the center of the park where a bandstand filled the clearing, its roof, a soft round shadow against the night sky. Jerry looked up. "Here it comes!" He pointed at the circling lights that slowly floated into view over the clearing.

The spaceship dipped slightly, and the lights reflected along its curved metal surface. Slowly it came to a stop directly above the bandstand roof. The hatch underneath slid open and the silver-colored wand began to descend with a little man in a metallic-colored suit clinging to it. He stepped to the roof, slid to the edge, gave a jump, and floated to the ground. As before, his bubble helmet reflected the lights above, and Jerry couldn't see his face. The spaceman turned slowly until his blinking blue light shone in the direction of the children.

"Come on, let's go," Jerry said and tried to hop forward. But his two sisters stood rooted to the ground, their eyes wide with astonishment.

Jerry tugged forward impatiently. "Don't be scared, that's just Monaal. He won't hurt us."

Hesitantly, the girls moved forward with Jerry supported between them.

A strange urgent beeping sound suddenly came from the spaceship. As the children neared the spaceman, he began to back away.

"It's only me, Monaal," Jerry reassured. But the spaceman bent forward and with a leap, floated to the bandstand roof.

"Monaal, please don't be frightened. I'm Jerry, remember? You talked with me . . . and I've brought the gismo, like you asked me to."

Monaal's answer was a sharp tap on the wand of the spaceship. He rode upward, the hatch slid closed, and with a high whine, the spaceship tilted to one side and rose rapidly toward the stars.

"Now why did he run away this time!" Jerry exclaimed.

"Maybe we frightened him," Lou said.

"Yeah," Dodie said. "Maybe he thought we had three heads and six feet."

"Oh, Dodie!" Jerry sighed. "We'd better go home. He won't be back again tonight."

"Are you sure?" Lou asked.

"Well, he didn't come back again last night."

The girls swung around, and Jerry hopped between them down the echoing sidewalk toward Park Street. They were nearly there when they saw the white form of a large street sweeper parked beside the curb. They could hear voices coming toward them.

Quickly, Lou pulled Jerry and Dodie behind the dark branches of a holly bush beside the walk.

Two men in coveralls clicked by. "So the street sweeper stalled! That's not so unusual, Charlie."

"But I tell you it was that . . . that *thing* up there did it when it flew over us." The second voice sounded shaken.

"Looked like it stopped about over the bandstand, didn't it?"

"Yeah, right about here." The two men paused in the clearing.

"Well, it isn't here now, that's for sure!"

The children could hear the voices coming back.

"This is the second night that thing's been around, Bill."

"Yeah, I know. Look, Charlie, we'd better keep quiet about this. Folks would never believe us if we said we'd seen a flying saucer."

"You're right, Bill, they'd never believe us!" The two men walked by. The children heard the sweeper start and drone on down the street. As soon as it was out of sight, they hurried as fast as Jerry could hop across the street and up the driveway of their house. The lights were still on in the living room.

"Good!" Jerry whispered. "Dad and Mom are downstairs."

"But how are we going to get back inside?" Lou asked.

"Let's just walk in the front door," Dodie suggested.

"Are you crazy?" Jerry exclaimed. "They'd ask us all sorts of questions and find out about the spaceship. Remember, this is a secret just between us kids, and you're *not* to tell anyone. Promise, Dodie?"

"Okay, I promise," Dodie said.

But Jerry felt uneasy, somehow. Dodie's promises weren't too reliable. He would have to watch her.

11

Keeping Dodie quiet

The three stood under the maple tree in the dim light of the midnight stars. Jerry balanced on his good foot and leaned against the trunk. "I guess we'll have to get back in the house the same way we came out. Think you can reach that lower limb by yourself, Lou?"

"Sure, no problem," Lou whispered back.

"Then you and Dodie give me a lift to the first branch. If I don't have to jump, I can make it from there."

"I can't jump that high, either," Dodie said.

"Lou'll help you after I climb up," Jerry said. "Now everyone be real quiet! Lou, you and Dodie put your hands together and make a step," he ordered. Jerry leaned heavily on the girls' shoulders and hopped his good foot into their waiting hands. They lifted him up a short distance. He grabbed for the branch and swung himself onto it. He worked his way slowly up the tree to the branch overhanging the porch. He straddled this limb and inched along toward the roof, where he eased himself carefully onto the shingles.

He turned. "Okay, Lou," he whispered down, "lift Dodie up. I'll help her onto the roof."

Lou picked Dodie up around the middle, and she began to giggle. "Oh, be quiet, Dodie!" Jerry hissed down at her. Dodie tried hard to stop as she climbed up the maple branches, but on reaching Jerry she broke into a fresh burst of giggles.

Jerry cupped his hands roughly over her mouth. "Will you shut up?" he whispered fiercely. "If Mom and Dad hear us, we've had it! Now get back into the room!" Dodie turned and crept across the porch roof to Jerry's window. "Okay, Lou, come on up." Jerry beckoned to his older sister.

Lou jumped, caught the limb, and swung herself into the tree. In a few moments, she was safely on the roof beside Jerry. Together they turned and crawled back to the bedroom window. Lou helped Jerry in, climbed in herself, and hooked the screen.

Jerry sank to the floor. "We made it! Oh, man, what a night!"

Lou sat down beside him. "You said it. If I live to be a hundred, I'll never forget that spaceship and that weird little man."

Dodie plopped down on the rug between them. "Me neither!"

"Well, don't ever tell, Dodie," Jerry cautioned.

"I won't, I won't."

"Look," Jerry said, "be a good kid and go back to bed."

"Yes, hurry!" Lou said, "Mom and Dad have turned the television off."

Dodie jumped up and scampered across the hall.

While Jerry rolled onto his hands and knees and headed for his bed, Lou tiptoed to the door. She turned. "I'm sorry about sitting on you, Jerry, I didn't know. . . ."

"That's okay," Jerry heaved himself onto the bed.

"What are you going to do now? About the gismo, I mean?" Lou asked.

"I haven't figured out yet." Jerry put his head on his pillow. "You won't tell anybody about tonight, will you?"

"Are you kidding?" Lou exclaimed. "Nobody would believe me if I did. Oh, oh! Here they come. Gotta go."

Jerry raised his head. "Thanks for helping, Lou," he whispered.

The next morning Jerry hobbled downstairs to breakfast, late. He hadn't been able to lace his sneaker over the swollen ankle.

Mrs. Cole broke an egg into the skillet. "What's the matter with everyone this morning? Your eyes all look like burned holes in a blanket! Didn't any of you get enough sleep?"

Mr. Cole reached for the toast. "Morning, Jerry, what happened to your foot?"

Jerry sat down at the table. "Oh, nothing much, just turned it a little."

"Yeah!" Dodie took a big bite of toast. "He fell over his . . ."

"Dodie!" Jerry said loudly, glaring across the table at her.

96

His father looked up sharply at him.

Jerry caught his father's look. "Dodie," he growled, "You've got jam on your face."

"I know its early, Jerry," his father said, "but there's no need to talk roughly to your sister. By the way, young man, you forgot to put your bike away last night."

"Yeah, I *know*! . . . I mean, *I* know."

"If you want your things to last, Jerry, you'd better get into the habit of taking care of them. Your bike goes in the garage."

"Yes, sir." Jerry glanced sideways at Lou, who hid a smile behind a sip of cocoa.

His mother came to the table. "Let me see that foot, Jerry."

"It's okay, Mom, really it is."

She knelt beside his chair. "Let me see it."

He held his foot out.

His mother turned the pants leg up. "Why, you can't even tie your shoelace around that ankle! It's back to bed for you!"

"Oh, Mom!"

His mother eased his shoe off. "How on earth did you do a thing like that!"

Jerry glared across at Dodie. "I fell over . . . something, that's all." Lou joined in the glaring, and Dodie ducked her head.

"We'll soak that ankle after breakfast,

then get your weight off of it," his mother said. "You look like you could use a little rest anyway."

Jerry was glad his mother didn't ask him any more questions while she helped him upstairs, soaked his ankle, and tucked him back into bed. He hoped Lou would be able to keep Dodie quiet about what had happened the night before.

That afternoon Ron came up to visit Jerry. "Your mom says you hurt your ankle. What happened?"

"Where were *you* last night, Ron? Man, could we have used you!"

"It was that stupid alarm clock . . . didn't go off. Guess it wasn't set right or something."

"I figured as much!" Jerry nodded.

"But what happened to your ankle?" Ron asked. "Did you see Monaal?"

Jerry told him of the night's adventures. "I'd sure like to know why Monaal backed off that way," he finished.

"Yeah, it's weird!" Ron said.

Jerry sat up in bed. "Listen, go get your telephone and earphones, and we'll hook the gismo up right here!" He slapped his nightstand.

When Ron returned, they fastened the gismo carefully to the radio set and attached the earphones and telephone.

"Better close the door, Ron," Jerry said.

Ron was latching the door when Dodie pushed against it. Ron looked at Jerry. "You want your kid sister in here?" he asked.

"Heck, no!" Jerry said.

"Sorry, Dodie, you've got to stay out." Ron braced his foot against the door.

"You better let me in or I'll tell about last night!" Dodie yelled through the door.

"Brat!" Jerry exclaimed. "Okay, let her in."

Dodie bounced into the room. "I didn't tell anybody, Jerry. I wanted to, but I didn't tell."

"Good girl. Now sit down and be quiet. We've got to hear something." Jerry took the receiver off the hook.

There was a light knock on the door, and Lou stuck her head in the room. "Okay if I come in?"

"Sure," Jerry said, "Might as well, everyone else is in here."

Lou walked over and gazed down at the crystal set with the maze of wires attached to it. "Is that the gismo?" She pointed at the tiny wires glowing pink now.

Jerry nodded and signaled for quiet. "I'm trying to get Monaal. "This is Jerry Cole calling Base Ship Plymo . . . Jerry Cole calling Base Ship Plymo . . . come in, please."

Ron slid the earphones over his head.

"I want to listen, too," Dodie said.

Jerry motioned for her to be quiet.

"If you don't let me listen, I'll—"

Jerry rolled his eyes. "Go ahead, Ron, hook up my earphones and turn 'em so Dodie and Lou can listen."

Ron fastened Jerry's headset onto the crystal radio and turned the earphones out. Lou sat down beside Dodie, and they put their ears to the set.

"This is Jerry Cole calling Base Ship Plymo. . . . Come in, please." Jerry repeated.

Sudden static crackled. "This is Base Ship Plymo, go ahead."

"Monaal?"

"Yes, Jerry?"

"Why did you back away from us last night?"

"There were three of you, Jerry. Who were the others?"

"Oh, those were my sisters, Lou and Dodie."

"I thought we agreed no one but you and Ron were to meet me?"

"We did, sir, but I turned my ankle and couldn't walk, and Ron's alarm clock didn't work so he overslept, and I had to get my sisters to help me come to the park. Was it because of my sisters that you left?"

"No, Jerry, we detected a vehicle approaching."

"That must have been the street sweeper," Jerry exclaimed. "Did you stall their machine?"

"Only temporarily."

"Man, were they shook!" Jerry laughed. "They came looking for you after you left."

"We were afraid they would. Now listen closely, Jerry. Since it will take a little time for your injury to mend, we will delay our next trip. Take good care of yourself and the gismo, but don't try to contact us. We will be elsewhere in your galaxy. When your planet has turned six rotations, however, we will return."

"That's in six days, isn't it?" Jerry asked.

"Yes," Monaal answered, "halfway through darkness."

"Where will we meet you?"

"To make it easier, we will descend over your house and meet you outside. I hope your ankle will be better by then."

"Thanks, Mr. Monaal, it will be."

"And this next time, Jerry," Monaal spoke slowly, "*nothing* must go wrong . . . *nothing!*"

There was a flurry of static. "Mr. Monaal, sir?" Jerry said, but there was no answer. The gismo had faded back to silver.

12

Seven hundred years old?

Jerry put the receiver back on the hook and ran his fingers through his hair. "Darn! I'll never find out where Monaal comes from or how his spaceship gets here if he hangs up on me all the time!"

Ron took his headphones off. "Yeah, or how he learned our language."

Lou laid the headphones she shared with Dodie in her lap. "Maybe he doesn't want you to know."

Jerry shook his head. "It sure looks that way."

Dodie wandered over and picked the telephone up. She lifted the receiver off the hook. "Calling Base Ship Plymo . . . Base Ship Plymo . . . come in, please," she mimicked Jerry.

Jerry grasped at the phone. "Dodie! Don't fool around with that!"

Dodie moved out of his reach. "I just want to ask Monaal something."

Jerry leaned out of bed. "Well he isn't there anymore. Give me the phone!"

Dodie stretched the distance of the wires just beyond Jerry's reach. "Hi! Are you Mr. Monaal?" Dodie spoke into the phone. "I'm Dodie . . . Yes . . . Jerry's sister. . . I saw you the other night in the park, remember?"

"Hey!" Ron picked his earphones up. "She's talking with him!"

Jerry nearly fell out of bed. "Dodie, give it here!" Then he turned to Lou. "Quick, hand me that other headset!" Lou held the earphones so Jerry could listen, too.

Monaal was speaking again. "You were helping your brother?"

"Yes," Dodie nodded. "Mr. Monaal, you're so little. How old are you?"

"Dodie!" Jerry exclaimed, "That's not . . ."

"I'm seven hundred years old by our calendar."

"Seven hundred years old!" Dodie exclaimed. "Why are you so small, then?"

"The planet Throal, where I live, is beyond your galaxy. It is very old and very large, much larger than your planet, and many people live on it. We have grown smaller so that there will be enough space and food for everyone who wants to stay there."

"You mean you shrink everyone down to your size?"

"No, Dodie, over hundreds of years we have developed smaller bodies."

"Do you have families like ours?"

"Yes, we do."

"Do you have a little girl like me?"

"Yes, her name is Kaali."

"Oh, I like Kaali! How big is she?"

"Well," chuckled Monaal, "she's not as big as you are."

"Is she half as big as you are, Mr. Monaal?"

"Just about . . . maybe a bit smaller."

Dodie held her hand out to the height she remembered Monaal, then lowered her hand halfway. "Why then she'd be only two feet high! Oh, I'd like to see Kaali! Does she play hopscotch?"

"Dodie!" Jerry exclaimed. "Don't bother him with stupid questions like that! Ask him what makes his spaceships fly."

Dodie looked at Jerry. "You ask him your questions and I'll ask him mine!"

"Then give me the phone!" Jerry made another grab for it.

"No!" Dodie turned away from him. She spoke into the mouthpiece. "Does Kaali play bounce ball against your garage door?"

Monaal's voice had a smile in it. "She plays lots of games, but I'm not familiar with their names. I haven't been home for some time, but I will be seeing her soon."

"Then ask her if she likes to play hopscotch and bounce ball, will you, please?"

"I will."

"Good-bye."

"Good-bye, Dodie."

Dodie put the receiver on the hook and set the phone on Jerry's nightstand. "I like Mr. Monaal. He's a nice man."

Jerry laid the headset down and grabbed the telephone. "Mr. Monaal?" He clicked the receiver up and down, but no one answered.

106

He put the phone back and thumped his covers with his fists. "Why couldn't he answer me! Of all the dumb questions to ask him, Dodie! Hopscotch! Bounce ball! Why couldn't you ask him important things? Now we'll never learn anything from him!"

Lou stood up. "We learned where he comes from—the planet Throal in another galaxy—and why he's so little."

"Sure," Dodie agreed. "And he's got a family and a little girl named Kaali."

"Yeah," Ron added. "And he's seven hundred years old! Wow!"

"What's so important about that!" Jerry fumed.

Lou walked toward the door. "Well, for one thing, it proves that we're not the only planet in the universe with people on it."

"Sure," Ron said, "and if they can all live to be seven hundred years old, they must have figured out a lot of things, like how to get rid of diseases and accidents and war."

"Yes, but their spaceships," Jerry said. "What are they made out of? How do they fly? Why are they flying around the Earth? *That's* what *I* want to know. And thanks to Dodie, I won't find out till I see Monaal next Saturday midnight!"

"Why are you mad at me?" Dodie asked.

"You wouldn't give me back the phone when Monaal was talking, that's why!"

"He was talking to me!"

"He was talking to me before that!"

"Well, you were through!"

"I was not! The static came, he didn't answer, so I thought . . . Oh, skip it! Go on out and play hopscotch!" Jerry plunked back on his pillow and stared at the ceiling.

The six days of waiting was a long time for Jerry. He tucked the gismo far back in his underwear drawer, and took it out each morning when he dressed. Whenever he held it in his hand, he thought of another question he wanted to ask Monaal. His ankle improved rapidly, and soon he was pedaling to and from school.

Friday afternoon Jerry coasted up the driveway with Ron just behind him. With his bike parked in the garage, Jerry shuffled beside Ron who was wheeling his own bike toward the hole in the hedge. Jerry stuffed his hands in his pockets. "Well, tomorrow night is UFO night!"

"Yeah!" Ron exclaimed. "Only it should be IFO—*Identified* flying object."

Jerry grinned. "I bet we're the only ones around here who can say that."

"Sure we are!" Ron agreed. "And when

we get through asking Monaal a bunch of questions tomorrow night, we'll be smarter than the space program guys!"

"Yeah, maybe." Jerry stopped at the hedge. "Look, how are you going to wake up, Ron, if your alarm clock doesn't work?"

"Oh, it works okay," Ron answered. When I set it last time, I forgot to pull out the knob on the back. Don't worry, I won't miss being over here this time!"

Saturday night, when his alarm went off under his pillow, Jerry was out of bed and into his clothes in a matter of seconds. He opened his chest of drawers softly, and pulling the gismo out, dropped it into his pocket. He stuffed his arms into his jacket and zipped it up. Quickly he crossed to the door and stood in the hall listening to the mutter of the Saturday night movie on the television. It was obviously the middle of a scene. If he was fast, he could make it downstairs and through the kitchen before the commercial.

Jerry tiptoed softly down the steps and through the hallway. He crossed the kitchen and was almost to the back porch when the kitchen light snapped on.

"Jerry! Just a minute. Where are you going?" It was his father!

13

But I promised Monaal–

Jerry blinked in the sudden brightness of the kitchen light. Why couldn't he have been a little quicker, he thought. He forced a smile. "Hi, Dad, I'm just going outside for a few minutes. "Be right back." He turned toward the back porch.

"Do you know what time it is, Jerry?" His father pointed at the kitchen clock. "Look!"

"Sure, I know . . . almost midnight. I've got to meet someone then."

"Who?" his father asked.

"Nobody you know, Dad."

"I don't like this, Jerry."

"It's okay, honest. I've got to give this gismo back." Jerry took the gismo from his pocket.

"Oh, then you found out who it belongs to?"

"Sure."

"By the way, just what is it?"

"A communication system."

"To what?"

Jerry dropped his eyes. "I can't tell you. You wouldn't believe me."

"What makes you think I wouldn't?"

Jerry looked up. "Because . . . well, because grown-ups think there's a logical explanation for everything."

"Isn't there?"

"Not for this gismo!" Jerry cupped it in his hand. "Look, Dad, I've got to go outside!"

"Just a minute, Son!" His father came towards him. "What's so mysterious about the gismo?"

"Well, it's . . . it's from a spaceship!"

"How do you know?"

"That's a long story, Dad, I'll tell you

later. Right now I've got to give this gismo back."

"Back to who?"

"Monaal, the spaceman."

"Spaceman! Now see here, Jerry, this has gone far enough! Just why do you want to go outside at midnight? Tell me the truth!"

"I have, Dad!" Jerry protested. "I've got to give this gismo back to Monaal. It's a communication system that fell off of some spacecraft named XR. Monaal's out there waiting for me right now!"

"You think I'll believe this?" His father's voice was beginning to sound angry.

"Dad, honest, I'm telling the truth! Come outside and see for yourself! The spaceship should be hovering over the house right now." Jerry ran for the back door and his father strode after him.

Even as he ran down the back steps, Jerry could hear the strange buzzing like a swarm of bees directly over his forehead. He backed away from the house and looked up. The soft whine of the motor floated down, but tonight no circling red and white lights glinted on the convex bottom. Only the great circle of the spaceship, like an enormous black shadow as large as the house, blotted out the stars.

"See, Dad, there it is!" Jerry pointed to the bobbing shape.

Ron came running from the hole in the hedge. "They just came down, Jerry." Then Ron saw Mr. Cole, and whispered into Jerry's ear, "Hey, how come your dad's here?"

"I couldn't get out of the house without him," Jerry whispered back.

Mr. Cole stood rooted to the ground. His mouth gaped open at the great dark spaceship floating over the house. Suddenly he seized both boys by their arms. His voice was urgent. "Into the house, both of you."

"But Dad! I promised Monaal . . ."

Mr. Cole paid no attention to Jerry's protest, but hurried the boys up the back steps and into the house. He walked them through the hallway and into the living room where Mrs. Cole was trying vainly to clear the heavy snow on the television set. He plunked the two boys onto the couch. "Turn the television off, Alice, I want you to hear this." He pulled a chair up and sat facing the boys, and held his hand out. "Jerry, let me have that gismo." His voice shook a little as he spoke.

Jerry handed the gismo to his father.

"Now," his father commanded, "I want you to tell me everything you've found out about the gismo—everything, do you hear?"

The boys looked at each other. The authority in Mr. Cole's voice was unshakeable. They couldn't keep the secret of the gismo any longer. Their words tumbled over one another as Jerry and Ron told of their experiments with the gismo . . . of their conversations with Monaal . . . of their two meetings with the spacemen. Mr. and Mrs. Cole listened intently.

"And now, Dad," Jerry finished, "please give me the gismo so I can return it to Monaal. I promised him I would."

Mr. Cole looked at the gismo, then at Jerry. "Do you know how important this piece of metal is, Jerry?"

"Of course I do!" Jerry replied.

His father looked earnestly into Jerry's face. "This gismo can unlock the secrets of the universe that have been puzzling our scientists for ages!"

"I know, Dad, but I promised Monaal, and we've got questions to ask him."

"This should be in the hands of our space engineers. *They* are the ones who should be asking the questions, not a couple of boys!" Mr. Cole said and looked at his watch. "If we leave now we can be at the U.S. Air Force base by morning." He turned to Mrs. Cole. "I'm taking the boys with me. The authorities will probably want to question them."

"Mr. Cole," Ron said, "Lou and Dodie saw the spaceship, and Dodie talked with Monaal, too."

"Then they must go along with us. Alice, wake the girls and get them ready. Dodie can rest in Jerry's sleeping bag in back of the station wagon."

It was nearly one o'clock in the morning when Mr. Cole herded everyone onto the front porch. The girls giggled and shivered as Mr. Cole made them wait while he peered cautiously up. But the spaceship was gone, and he beckoned for everyone to hurry to the garage.

Mr. Cole backed the car out and headed down Park Street. Jerry sat beside his father and watched the headlights tunnel into the night. "Dad?"

"Yes, Jerry?"

"Could I please hold the gismo . . . just till we get there?"

"Yes, I guess so. It's in my coat pocket next to you."

Jerry reached in his father's pocket and drew the gismo out. He held it in one hand and stroked the furlike wires on top. Where was the spaceship now, he wondered. What did

Monaal think of him, especially when he had said "nothing must go wrong, this time, nothing," and everything had! His father was right about the gismo unlocking the secrets of the universe, but was it fair to use it this way after Jerry had promised to give it back? To break a promise to someone—even someone from another planet—wasn't right. He wished he had never found the gismo!

It was quiet as they drove through the long night. Lou and Ron dozed in the back seat. Dodie bounced about adjusting the sleeping bag in the rear of the station wagon. Mr. Cole seemed lost in thought, and Jerry was too miserable to say anything. He sat staring at the gismo.

The highway they followed, deserted now in the early hours before dawn, lay across long stretches of cornfields and low, rolling pasture land. They had come to a rise in the road, when the car motor died suddenly, the lights went out, and the station wagon rolled to a stop.

Jerry leaned forward. "What's wrong, Dad?"

His father tried to start the car, but nothing happened. "I don't know Jerry, the electrical system is out, I guess."

A familiar buzzing sound directly over

Jerry's forehead made him sit up. He looked at his father with wide eyes. "I know why it stalled," he said in a low voice.

"Why?" his father asked.

"The spaceship is over us!"

14

The new Gismo

Straining against his seat belt, Jerry leaned forward and peered out of the windshield. He pointed up. "Look, Dad!"

His father leaned forward, too, then drew his breath in. Circling red and white lights floated above them reflecting on the car hood. The spaceship drew ahead of them and hovered above the asphalt road. At the bottom of the ship, the hatch slid open and the silver wand descended slowly. A dozen little men clung to it, the blue lights on their chests blinking. When the wand touched the road, the men jumped off and, spreading out into a half circle, walked toward the car.

Lou, Ron, and Dodie awakened by the sudden stop, stared wide-eyed at the approaching spacemen.

One figure separated from the others and stepped forward.

"It's Monaal!" Jerry exclaimed. "He's come for the gismo!" Jerry turned to his father. "Dad, I know you have a point about keeping the gismo, but I've *got* to give it back." He unfastened his seat belt, slid across the seat, and opened the car door.

"I'll go with you, Jerry." His father followed him, while Ron, Lou, and Dodie piled out of the back seat. They stood by the side of the road, a circle of blinking blue lights surrounding them.

Monaal lifted the front of his space helmet. In the dim light of the sky just before dawn, Jerry looked into a kind and smiling face of a handsome little man. His voice was high-pitched and friendly. "I hope we didn't frighten you too much, but it was most necessary we contact you."

"That's okay, Mr. Monaal," Jerry said.

"I'm sorry I couldn't meet you back at my house, but, ah . . . things came up I hadn't figured on."

Monaal nodded. "I thought so."

"This is my father, Mr. Cole," Jerry said.

The spaceman bowed ever so slightly. "It's a pleasure to meet the father of such an intelligent boy."

Mr. Cole reached down and shook Monaal's hand. "Thank you, sir."

"And this is Ron and Lou and Dodie." Jerry motioned to each in turn. Monaal greeted each one with a bow.

Dodie squeezed between Jerry and Mr. Cole. "Hi, Mr. Monaal. I'm Dodie, remember?"

Monaal smiled warmly at her. "Yes, indeed, I remember you. I saw my own little girl, Kaali, over our intergalactic communication screen, and I told her about you."

"Did you ask her about hopscotch and bounce ball?"

"Yes, but she calls them by different names."

"Oh, I wish I could play hopscotch with Kaali! We could have lots of fun together."

"I'm sure you could," Monaal smiled and turned to Jerry. "I think you know why we're here."

120

Jerry nodded. "Yes, sir, you came for the gismo."

Monaal looked up at Mr. Cole. "I'm sure you'll agree with me that the gismo is *not* a child's toy."

Mr. Cole nodded vigorously. "I certainly do!"

Jerry held the gismo tightly in his fist. "Before I give the gismo back, sir, would you please answer a few questions for me?"

"If I can, Jerry," Monaal said.

"What makes your spacecraft go?"

"It travels on what we call 'a universal current,' a magnetic power found throughout the universe. That's as much as I can tell you now, Jerry. Your own scientists will be discovering it soon."

"And how did you learn to speak our language?" Jerry asked.

Ron leaned forward. "Yes, sir, how?"

Monaal laughed. "That's an easy question. I didn't have to."

"You mean people on your planet speak the same language we do?" Jerry exclaimed.

"Oh, no, we don't. Open your hand, Jerry, and look at the gismo," Monaal ordered.

Jerry uncurled his fingers and gazed in astonishment at the tiny wires on top of the gismo. They glowed cherry red. He looked up. "How come? It's not attached to anything."

"Those tiny antennae on top don't need to be. They are language converters."

"Language converters!" Jerry and Ron spoke at once.

"Yes. You see, as I speak, they convert the vibrations of my voice into sounds you are familiar with."

"Wow!" Ron whispered.

Jerry looked puzzled. "But I thought you said the gismo was a communications system from XR?"

"The bottom part is. That is why when you fastened its knobs to your circuit you were able to reach us."

Jerry gazed at the glowing wires in his hand. "And *that's* why the wires on top always turned red when we talked . . . they were converting the sound vibrations so we could understand each other!"

"Exactly, Jerry. You see, from our planet, Throal, we carry on trade with planets that have languages different from ours. We must be able to communicate."

"Are you going to carry on trade with our planet? Is that why you're flying around Earth?"

Monaal smiled and shook his head. "Your planet isn't ready for that yet."

"I don't see why not! We've landed on the moon already, and we'll be landing on Mars and Venus pretty soon."

"Yes, I know. But that's only the first step into space. Your inhabitants have much to learn before they're ready for interplanetary and intergalactic trade."

"Then why are you flying around Earth?" Jerry asked.

"To learn more about your continents, your oceans, your atmosphere, just as your spacemen will study other planets." Monaal held his hand out and smiled at Jerry.

Slowly Jerry handed the gismo to Monaal. "I wish I knew how to make a gismo like that myself," he sighed.

Monaal took the gismo and patted Jerry's arm. "You will, someday." He looked up at Mr. Cole. "A boy who can discover how to attach a space communication system to an improvised circuit and send messages with it will go far, I assure you!"

Mr. Cole smiled. "I hope so."

Monaal beckoned to the circle of men who clustered about him.

"We must take this to XR now," he said.

"Oh, then you found XR. Where was it?" Ron asked.

"Back on your natural satellite at crater 7, where most of our spacecraft make emergency landings." Monaal raised his hand. "Sorry, but we must go now. Good-bye, everyone." He started for the spaceship.

"'Good-bye," chorused Jerry, Ron, Lou, Dodie, and Mr. Cole.

The spacemen shuffled to the silver wand and clinging to it rose slowly into the spaceship. Monaal was the last one left on the platform. He paused just below the hatch. "I'll be talking with you again, Jerry," he shouted.

"When?" Jerry called eagerly.

"When you finish making your gismo!" Monaal waved, and the wand disappeared into the ship. The hatch closed, the revolving lights circled faster, and the spaceship rose swiftly into the lightening sky.

Everyone stood watching it until it became a speck. Then they turned and climbed slowly back into the station wagon, whose lights had blinked on meanwhile. Mr. Cole started the car, swung it around, and headed back toward Bridgeville. No one spoke for a long time.

At last Jerry turned to his father. "You know, Dad, nobody's going to believe what happened to us tonight."

Mr. Cole nodded. "You're right."

"Maybe we'd better not mention it to anyone," Jerry said.

"A good idea, Son, we'll just keep it to ourselves. Okay, everyone?"

The sky ahead of them was turning to gold. Jerry watched it grow brighter and brighter. High above the horizon he caught the sudden glint of sunlight on metal. It lasted a moment and was gone. He would miss Monaal . . . but only for a while . . . only until he finished making a gismo of his own!

About the Author

Keo Felker Lazarus, a UCLA graduate and mother of four, grew up on a lemon ranch in southern California. "Books, music, and writing," she says, "filled my spare time when I wasn't hiking or swimming or hunting Indian relics in the foothills with my brother."

Later, in her own household, there was no TV. The family carted home armloads of books from the library each week. "It was while reading to my children," she says, "that I became inspired to write for young people."

Rattlesnake Run was her first publication. Seven books have followed since then on subjects ranging from archaeology to space travel.

When asked why she writes for children, Mrs. Lazarus replies, "Children have given me so much pleasure over the years that I want to give them something in return."

Mrs. Lazarus lives with her husband, Professor Arnold Lazarus, in Santa Barbara, California. They have five grandchildren.